CONTENTS

Also available by Tony Bradman,
and published by Corgi Pups:

THE FRANKENSTEIN TEACHER

Series Reading Consultant: Prue Goodwin
Reading and Language Information Centre,
University of Reading

Shiver One

This is Sunny Bank Infant and Junior.

It looks like an ordinary school... It certainly *sounds* like an ordinary school... It smells like an ordinary school too, all musty and dusty and chalky, with wandering whiffs of school dinners and disinfectant.

And that's mostly what it is –
an ordinary school, a very
ordinary school indeed. But wait...
something *EXTRA*-ordinary is
about to happen here. Something
very strange, and very peculiar,
and very, very... *SPOOKY*!

Look... there by the dustbins,
what do you see? A shimmering
and a glimmering, and a figure
forming in the darkness.

It is The Ghost Teacher, and
her name is Miss Shade.

She glides over to a window, and peers in...

"Class Three! *Class Three!*" Somebody was trying hard to make herself heard above an absolutely terrible din. "Will you *please* be quiet and behave! I'm warning you, this is *definitely* your last chance..."

"Oh dear, things are much, much worse than I thought," whispered Miss Shade. "I only hope I'm not too late..."

Then she slid... *through* the wall and into the school. She drifted down a corridor...

wafted round a corner... then slipped through a keyhole. She was in the classroom where the absolutely terrible din was coming from.

Class Three

No-one there could see her...
not yet, anyway. But she could
see them. And Class Three were
doing what they did best –
behaving badly.

School
is

They got up to
the usual things,
of course –
dreaming when
they should be
working,

fidgeting
when they
should be
sitting still,

chattering
when they
should be
listening,

picking their noses
and flicking it
at each other.

They did much more, though.

They did lots
of pulling and
prodding
and poking.

They did lots
of crashing and
bashing and
practical joking.

They did lots
of fighting
and biting
and writing...

but only
on the wall.

This is what Class Three's classroom looked like at nine o'clock on the first morning of term.

This is what it looked like just *one hour* later.

14

And this is... what Class Three look like. They're shocking, aren't they?

Class Three made more noise than the rest of Sunny Bank Infant and Junior School put together. They were more trouble than a barrel full of babies. In short, Class Three were... a teacher's worst nightmare.

This is Miss Nicely, Class Three's teacher. She was trying to do what *she* did best – teaching Class Three all sorts of interesting stuff.

But Class Three, as usual, weren't taking any notice of her. And Miss Nicely was feeling fed up. She was fed up with shouting. She was fed up with not being listened to. She was very fed up with Class Three.

This is what
Miss Nicely
looked like at
nine o'clock
on the first
morning of term.

This is what
she looked
like just
one hour later.

And this
is an extreme
close-up of
what she
looks like
today. It's
shocking,
isn't it?

Suddenly, something snapped inside her.

She grabbed her handbag and headed towards the door. For once, Class Three *did* take notice.

"Hey, Miss!" they called out, rudely. "Where are you going?"

I'm leaving. And I'm not coming back!

Then she slammed the
door shut behind her, and
strode off down the corridor. Miss
Shade slid through the classroom
wall, and wafted along after Miss
Nicely. They could both hear
Class Three... cheering.

This is Mr Dickens, headteacher of Sunny Bank Infant and Junior.

He looks like an ordinary headteacher. He sounds like an ordinary headteacher. He smells like an ordinary headteacher too, all musty and dusty and chalky, with wandering whiffs of school dinners and disinfectant.

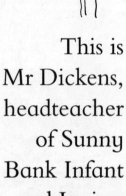

And that's exactly what he is,
an ordinary headteacher, a very
ordinary headteacher indeed.
At that precise moment he was
*head*ing down the corridor too,
and he was about to bump into
Miss Nicely.

"Not any more, there isn't,"
said Miss Nicely. "I resign, Mr
Dickens. You can find somebody
else to be Class Three's teacher
from now on."

And with that, she swept out
of the school.

A horrified Mr Dickens watched her go. He listened to Class Three creating havoc in the distance, and a frown crossed his face. Then he turned and marched off to his office, looking very, *very*... determined.

"Umm," murmured Miss Shade. "Time I got to work..."

Shiver Two

Miss Shade glided along the corridor to Class Three's classroom, where the din was even more terrible than before. She waited outside for a moment, listening and tutting. Then she slid in through the... *closed* door.

And this time she made sure everyone there could see her.

Class Three were rather surprised by her... *appearance*. In fact, they were so surprised, they stopped having a riot. They went very quiet indeed.

This is what they looked like before Miss Shade appeared.

And this is what they looked like
one second later. They froze in the
middle of whatever naughtiness
they were up to.

They look shocked, don't they?

"Good morning, Class Three,"

said Miss Shade. Class Three didn't reply, although some of them did close their mouths. "My name is Miss Shade, and I will be standing in for Miss Nicely. We've got lots to do, so..."

said somebody brave.

"Of course I am!" said Miss Shade. There was a sharp intake of breath from the entire class. "Now, settle down, everybody," continued Miss Shade. "I'm going to..."

The entire class trembled...

...tell you a story.

Class Three
stopped trembling,
and breathed out
in relief.

What k-k-k-kind
of story, Miss?

said the brave child.

A... scary one.
Are you ready?

She clicked her ghostly fingers,
and it went dark. Strange,
haunting noises filled the air.
Peculiar wisps of light appeared
from everywhere.

And Miss Shade gave off
a...*spooky* glow.

N-n-n-no
we're
not!

everybody in Class Three wailed.
They hugged each other in fright,
but Miss Shade took absolutely no
notice of them.

"Once upon a time,"
she said, in a voice
that made the little
hairs stand up on
the backs of the
children's necks,
"there was a school,
a very ordinary
school.

But in that
school there was a
badly behaved class..."

As Class Three watched, the wall behind Miss Shade turned blurry, began to fade, then vanished completely. A phantom classroom appeared, and with a gasp, Class Three recognized the people in it straightaway.

"Hey, *that's us!*" they yelled,
amazed.

"In fact, they were absolutely
awful," continued Miss Shade.
"They never allowed their poor,
poor teacher a moment's peace.
They misbehaved the whole time.
And I'm sorry to say they did some
terrible things..."

The phantom classroom before Class Three wobbled, and changed. Soon Class Three were watching something like a film on fast forward. And they saw everything they had got up to since the first day of term.

They saw all the pulling and prodding and poking. They saw all the crashing and bashing and practical joking. They saw all the fighting and biting. And they definitely saw all the writing on the wall.

None of them said a word. But as they sat there in the darkness watching themselves, some of Class Three *did* feel slightly... ashamed.

Their poor, poor teacher always tried hard to make the lessons interesting.

The phantom film slowed, then cut to a vision of Miss Nicely working at home.

"But the class didn't give a hoot."

Now some more of Class Three felt quite... ashamed.

"Then one day," said Miss Shade, "the class behaved *so* badly, their poor, poor teacher couldn't stand it a minute longer. She left, and started looking for another job, any job... provided it didn't involve children."

At last, the whole of Class Three felt very ashamed indeed. Although that didn't stop one or two of them from still being rather... cheeky.

"Here, Miss!" a voice called out. "This story isn't very scary!"

"Don't worry," said Miss Shade. "We're just getting to the scary part... The head of the school had to find someone to replace the poor, poor teacher.

So he decided to put an advertisement in the newspaper."

The vision of Miss Nicely
wobbled, and changed into a
picture of Mr Dickens writing at
his desk:

NEW TEACHER
WANTED AT
SUNNY BANK SCHOOL
MUST BE
VERY, VERY,
VERY STRICT.

Mr Dickens

Then the phantom picture
went into fast forward again.

Class Three watched as the newspaper was printed, teachers read the advertisement and replied, then came to be interviewed for the job by Mr Dickens. "Finally, the head found the person he was looking for," said Miss Shade. "Someone who would keep you under control, someone who wouldn't stand for any nonsense. In short, Class Three – your worst nightmare..." Class Three gulped at the vision before them.

Shiver Three

It was a teacher with a beaky nose and an even beakier chin. It was a teacher with a tight little bun and an even tighter little mouth. It was a teacher with steely blue eyes that saw... *everything*.

And her name was... *Miss Stern*. A phone rang in the phantom film. Miss Stern reached out and answered it. Her voice made Class Three instantly sit up straight.

Miss Stern put the phone down, and slowly turned to stare at Class Three. The phantom film froze with her eyes drilling into them. A few of the children – probably the cheeky ones – let slip little moans.

Please, Miss, tell us it isn't true!

"I only wish I could," said Miss Shade, sadly. "But alas, I can't. You have seen your past, Class Three, and what is happening in the present. You have also seen your future, and that cannot be changed. Unless..."

"Unless what, Miss?" several voices called out, eagerly.

"Unless," said Miss Shade, "you change... *yourselves*. You *could* give up the pulling and prodding and poking, the crashing and bashing and practical joking, and the fighting and biting and writing on the wall..."

"We can't!" said a voice. "We *love* doing that stuff! It's what we do best, isn't it, everybody?"

There was much murmuring of agreement.

"Oh well," said Miss Shade with a sigh.

"If that's the way you feel, I won't argue. But you'd better get used to how things are going to be..." Miss Shade clicked her ghostly fingers.

49

Suddenly, Miss Stern's phantom
film face came to life once more.

"Right, Class Three!" she snapped.
"Silence! No play-time until you've
finished all the difficult sums..."

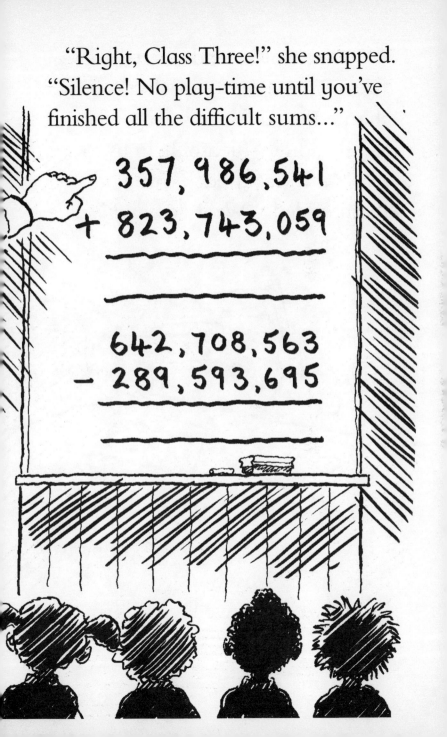

$$357,986,541$$
$$+ \ 823,743,059$$

$$642,708,563$$
$$- \ 289,593,695$$

"OK, we surrender!" yelled Class Three, remembering too the shame they'd felt at seeing what they'd done. "Please, help us to get Miss Nicely back," one of them added. "We'll do *anything* you say."

"Cross your hearts and hope to die?" asked Miss Shade.

"If we don't, we'll eat worm pie!" chanted Class Three.

"I'm glad to hear it," said Miss Shade, clicking her ghostly fingers again. The darkness was replaced by light, and the wall returned to normal. "Right, you can make a start by tidying this classroom. It's a *disgrace*..." Class Three set to work with a will.

This is what the classroom
looked like when they began.

This is what it looked like just
one hour later.

And this is Class Three looking a bit shocked at being so well behaved.

"What do you think, Miss?" said somebody, proudly.

"I think you never know what you can do until you've tried, Class Three," replied Miss Shade. "Wouldn't you agree? Now I want you all to sit down, fold your arms, and prepare to say something very important."

Miss Shade
clicked her fingers
one last time.
Soft, sprinkly, tinkling
sounds came from everywhere,
and then... a dazed Miss Nicely
appeared out of thin air. Miss
Shade made sure Miss Nicely
couldn't see her.

"Oh, no," Miss Nicely groaned, and closed her eyes. "I can't stand it!"

"Come on, Class Three," whispered Miss Shade. "Say the magic words..."

"*Sorry*, Miss Nicely!" said someone. Other voices joined in, and soon the whole of Class Three was apologizing.

Please be our teacher!
We won't be horrible any more.
Make up, make up,
never, never break up...

Miss Nicely opened her eyes. She looked as if she'd just woken from her worst nightmare. She smiled, faintly.

Then Mr Dickens came in.

"Ah, you're back, Miss Nicely," he said, and dropped a crumpled piece of paper in the bin. "I see you've got everything under control here, too. Nicely done, Miss Nicely. Keep up the good work, Class Three!"

"I couldn't have put it better myself," whispered Miss Shade. She smiled, waved goodbye... and slipped out through the keyhole.

"Who said that?" asked Mr Dickens.

But nobody told him...

That's more or less the end of
this story. Class Three *did* keep up
the good work, except for some
dreaming and fidgeting and
chattering and nose
picking and flicking.
Miss Nicely didn't
mind all that,
though.

She wasn't *quite* sure what had happened. But compared to how they'd been before, Class Three were... *angels*, so she wasn't complaining.

And what, you ask, became of
Miss Shade? Well, as long as
there's a class misbehaving
somewhere, there's no rest for
The Ghost Teacher.

Which means the next school
to get a SPOOKY visit is...
BOUND TO BE YOURS!

The End